D1592189

Natalie, Michelle, Christina, and Victoria. God blessed me
with the joy of seeing you four girls become more than
I could've ever imagined. Your love and example have
inspired me to continue to breakthrough my own limiting
beliefs and go after my dreams. I love you each so very much!
~Mom

It has been a joy to be a part of this lovely project.
The meaningful details, feelings, and story
have made it a unique and wonderful journey.
AND I got to learn how to make a perfect apple pie.
~Cennet

To contact the author https://jillwolf.mykajabi.com/LauraWasson
To contact the illustrator https://jillwolf.mykajabi.com/CennetKapkac
To contact the publisher https://jillwolf.mykajabi.com/29MinutesPublishing
7575 Emerald Stars Ave. Unit 102, North Las Vegas, NV 89084

ISBN: 979-8-9859475-3-3

Ballet, Pies and First Tries

Written By
Laura Wasson

Illustrated By
Cennet Kapkac

Laulee burst into Gram's house and what did she spy?
Her wonderful grandma was baking some pie!

2

Gram smiled and said, "I'm almost done! I waited for you to have some pie fun."

3

"When I was your age my mom showed me how
To finish a crust that would make people WOW!
It's a neat trick with two thumbs and one finger
Let's get started... no reason to linger."

4

Gram showed her how with fingers just right
To go 'round the crust edge, pressing it tight.

5

Gram's crust looked amazing! Laulee gave it a go
And when she was finished stepped back and said, "WHOA!"

"I give it an 'F' since it's all wonky!
It looks like my crust was made by a monkey!"

7

"You give yourself an 'F' on your very first try?
Is it really a failure? Can you explain why?"
"I guess I wanted it to look just like yours
Or maybe even like the crust in the stores!"

"Look over there by my recipe file,
It's my first crust, " Gram said with a smile.

Laulee looked at it closely, then grinned ear to ear,
"Mine looks like yours!" She twirled with a cheer.

Ballet class was scheduled for later that week.
Laulee was sure there'd be little to tweak.
She loved to practice all the things she'd been taught.
I'll get an "A" is what she had thought.

After warm-up and stretching, when Miss Hayley said, "Let's learn something new." Laulee's heart filled with dread.

Miss Hayley leaned forward, spread her arms out like wings
And lifted her leg back. It was a beautiful thing.

"It's perfectly lovely!" said Laulee enthralled.
"An arabesque is what this is called.
It's all about balance, now it's your turn."
It seems way too hard, Laulee thought with concern.

With her hand on the bar, she leaned forward just so,
Lifted her leg back and pointed her toe.

14

Unstable she wobbled and with a frown on her face
Said, "I give this an 'F' for balance and grace!"
Very surprised, Miss Hayley stepped back.
"Really? An 'F'? You're just getting the knack."

15

"A few years ago, when I was
your age,
I lost my balance and fell on the
stage."

"It's true this is my very first try.
It sort of reminds me of Gram
and the pie.

"Then it's an 'E' for EFFORT and a new attitude! I'll keep on practicing until it is good!"

17

Saturday, Quinnie came over to play.
Laulee suggested they make creatures with clay.

They each had their clump. What could they make?
Quinnie chose a kangaroo. Laulee chose a snake.

19

They smooshed and they smashed.

They pushed and they pulled.

20

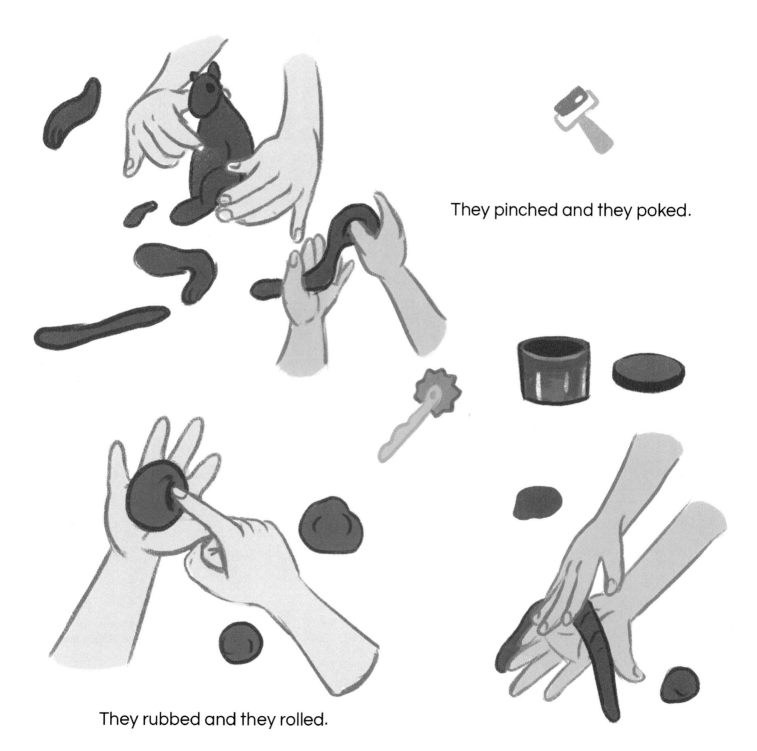

They pinched and they poked.

They rubbed and they rolled.

21

They grinned and they giggled, then came to a stop
As they saw what they'd formed... each seemed a flop.
"My snake looks more like a worm," Laulee said,
As she tossed it aside and it fell on its head.

"At least your worm isn't a goofy eyesore.
My kangaroo looks like a strange dinosaur."

Then Laulee thought of the pie
and ballet.
Why strive for an "A" when we're
playing with clay?

23

"Playing with you and the clay has been fun.
Since that was our goal, I think we have WON!"
"You are right, Laulee! That is so true.
And the very best part is being with you!"

24

"Let's look again with joy as our aim.
Mine's kind of cute, I'll give him a name!
How about Snorm? He's a snake-worm today.
He'll be something else next time, he's made out of clay!"

25

Quinnie laughed and said, "I'll name mine Boris! A large-headed, big-eyed, blue Kangasaurus!"

Enjoy your first tries!

Laura Wasson

Made in the USA
Columbia, SC
01 February 2023